To Jordan
—G.M.

For peace
—S.W.

**Go to www.scholastic.com for web site information
on Scholastic authors and illustrators.**

Text copyright © 2000 by Grace Maccarone.
Illustrations copyright © 2000 by Sam Williams.
All rights reserved. Published by Scholastic Inc.
SCHOLASTIC and associated logos are trademarks and/or registered trademarks of Scholastic Inc.

Library of Congress Cataloging-in-Publication Data
Maccarone, Grace.
     A child was born: a first nativity book / by Grace Maccarone ; illustrated by Sam Williams.
       p.   cm.
     Summary: Rhyming text retells the story of the birth of Jesus.
     ISBN 0-439-18296-4 (hardcover)
     1. Jesus Christ—Nativity—Juvenile literature. [1. Jesus Christ—Nativity. 2. Christmas. 3. Bible stories—N.T.]
I. Williams, Sam, ill. II. Title.
BT315.2 .M2 3   2000
232.92—dc21   99-088022

12 11 10 9 8 7 6 5 4 3 2 1   00 01 02 03 04

Printed in Mexico   49
First printing, November 2000

A CHILD WAS BORN

A First Nativity Book

by Grace Maccarone
Illustrated by Sam Williams

SCHOLASTIC INC.

New York Toronto London Auckland Sydney Mexico City New Delhi Hong Kong

Long ago,
there was a tax
on each man's worth,

so each returned
to the place of his birth.

Mary and Joseph
arrived at night,
in a city asleep
and locked up tight.

Tired and worn,
they went to the inn—
no room for her,
no room for him.

Instead,
they slept in a shed—
straw for a bed—

with a mare, a cow,
a ewe, and a sow.

A Newborn cried,
His mother sighed.

Shepherds feared
as angels appeared.

Hearing news of joy—
the birth of a Boy—
the shepherds set off
to visit the Child
asleep in a trough.

For all they had seen,
for all they had heard,

they thanked the Lord,
then spread the word.

And Three Wise Men
traveled far,

by the light of a star,

to bring
gifts for a King

and to celebrate
His glorious birth.

This Child was born
to save the earth.